TO WILLEM ROSENTHAL AND JULIA KOSTREVA,
FOR THEIR ENCOURAGEMENT AND SPOT-ON CRITICISM

ATHENEUM BOOKS FOR
YOUNG READERS • AN IMPRINT OF SIMON & SCHUSTER
CHILDREN'S PUBLISHING DIVISION • 1230 AVENUE OF THE AMERICAS,
NEW YORK, NEW YORK 10020 • TEXT COPYRIGHT © 2012 BY EILEEN ROSENTHAL
• ILLUSTRATIONS COPYRIGHT © 2012 BY MARC ROSENTHAL • ALL RIGHTS RESERVED,
INCLUDING THE RIGHT OF REPRODUCTION IN WHOLE OR IN PART IN ANY FORM. • ATHENEUM
BOOKS FOR YOUNG READERS IS A REGISTERED TRADEMARK OF SIMON & SCHUSTER, INC. •
FOR INFORMATION ABOUT SPECIAL DISCOUNTS FOR BULK PURCHASES, PLEASE CONTACT SIMON &
SCHUSTER SPECIAL SALES AT 1-866-506-1949 OR BUSINESS@SIMONANDSCHUSTER.COM. • THE
SIMON & SCHUSTER SPEAKERS BUREAU CAN BRING AUTHORS TO YOUR LIVE EVENT. FOR MORE
INFORMATION OR TO BOOK AN EVENT, CONTACT THE SIMON & SCHUSTER SPEAKERS BUREAU
AT 1-866-248-3049 OR VISIT OUR WEBSITE AT WWW.SIMONSPEAKERS.COM. • BOOK
DESIGN BY DAN POTASH • THE TEXT FOR THIS BOOK IS SET IN P22 POP ART •
THE ILLUSTRATIONS FOR THIS BOOK ARE DRAWN IN PENCIL AND COLORED
DIGITALLY • MANUFACTURED IN CHINA • 0112 SCP • FIRST EDITION •
2   4   6   8   10   9   7   5   3   1
CIP DATA FOR THIS BOOK IS AVAILABLE
FROM THE LIBRARY OF CONGRESS.
ISBN 978-1-4424-0378-9 (HC)
ISBN 978-1-4424-3534-6
(EBOOK) --------

- - - - -
--

I'LL SAVE YOU BOBO!

EILEEN ROSENTHAL

ILLUSTRATED BY MARC ROSENTHAL

ATHENEUM BOOKS FOR YOUNG READERS

NEW YORK   LONDON   TORONTO   SYDNEY   NEW DELHI

WILLY IS HAVING A HARD TIME READING. . . .

GO AWAY, EARL.

EARL!

EARL, NO!
GO AWAY!

LOOK, BOBO! THE BIG DINOSAUR
IS GOING TO EAT THE LITTLE DINOSAUR!

RATS! HE JUST EATS TREES.
THIS STORY'S NO GOOD.

LET'S WRITE OUR OWN BOOK, BOBO.
IT WILL BE ALL ABOUT YOU. AND ME.

BOBO, YOU'LL HAVE A SCARY ADVENTURE.
AND I'LL SAVE YOU.

ONCE UPON A TIME WE WERE IN A JUNGLE.
EVERYTHING IS REALLY BIG. AND GREEN.

BOBO, THAT'S WHERE MONKEYS COME FROM,
BUT THERE ARE NO MONKEYS THIS TIME,
ONLY YOU AND ME.

THERE ARE BIG, ENORMOUS TREES.

AND THAT ONE HAS
A SNAKE IN IT!

THEY HAVE SNAKEY
RED TONGUES, AND
THERE ARE GIANT
POISON MUSHROOMS.

AND WE HAVE A TENT!

BOBO, DON'T MOVE, I'LL BE RIGHT BACK.

EARL! NO CATS ALLOWED IN THE TENT.

THIS JUNGLE HAS LOTS OF FIERCE WILD ANIMALS,
BUT BOBO IS SO BRAVE, HE WANTS TO LOOK AROUND. . . .

THAT'S YOU, BOBO.

HE DOESN'T KNOW THERE ARE TIGERS!
AND THEY HAVE BIG TEETH.

BOBO, DON'T GO UP IN
THAT SNAKE TREE!

THE TIGER IS CLIMBING THE TREE. AND BOBO DOESN'T SEE HIM.

I'LL SAVE YOU, BOBO!

YAAA!

HELP! BOBO!

EARL!

YOU WRECKED OUR STORY!

COME ON, BOBO, WE'RE MOVING.

ONCE UPON A TIME NOW, WE'RE
IN A DIFFERENT JUNGLE.

THIS ONE HAS MORE SNAKES. AND VINES.
VERY SNAKEY VINES.

AND A BIG SNAKE IS ABOUT TO EAT EARL ALIVE.

RAHR!

AND HE ATE HIM.
THE END.

YES.

SNAKE BOOKS ARE ALWAYS GOOD, BOBO.

SNAKE!

OH EARL.